BEYOND YOUR COMFORT ZONE

A KID'S SECRET GUIDE TO FACING HOMESICKNESS

By Tracy Bryan

"I'm continually trying to make choices that put me against my own comfort zone. As long as you're uncomfortable, it means you're growing."
Ashton Kutcher

(c) 2015 Tracy Bryan
tracybryan.com

Image Rights Purchased From Shutterstock.com

BEYOND YOUR COMFORT ZONE

A KID'S SECRET GUIDE TO FACING HOMESICKNESS

By Tracy Bryan

Imagine this..
The summer is just about here, school is almost over and your ready to relax...but your parents just signed you up for camp! What? Yikes!

If it's your first time going to camp, there must be many questions that you have floating around in your head...the most common one is- what if I get HOMESICK?

There are a lot of kids1 that spend at least a part- if not all- of their summer at camp and believe it or not, almost all kids get homesick, especially if it's their first time away.

Everyone feels a little homesick when they are away from familiar things like family, pets and friends. It's a natural human reaction, some people just feel it more than others!

What is HOMESICKNESS?

Just saying the word slowly (home/sickness) will tell you what it's all about, but the REASON why we get it explains the definition of it much better. Heres why we get homesick...

In your home, there are so many familiar people, objects and situations that you get used to in your everyday life. When you first wake up in the morning, you jump out of YOUR BED, in YOUR ROOM, in YOUR HOUSE. These are all plain objects that you have made familiar to you- their yours. The same way that an empty house becomes a home to the people living it or an animal that you've adopted becomes your pet, your family.

These start off as everyday stuff, but when we have a connection to them, they become part of our life, part of us. When we go without them, it can feel like something is missing in our life, missing in us.

As much as we don't like to place value on "things", they do have importance in our life. Have you ever heard the saying- "the important things in life aren't things, they are people." ? That's true, people are more important than anything, but it's still human to want to connect with the things around us, to make them our own.

We have to make these things our own in order to live comfortably in this world. We possess things- that's why we have money- to be able to buy the things that we need in our life. We buy things that make our life more comfortable...like a house, a bed, etc. Take these away and we are left with a lot of space and nothing to sleep on! It would be like camping...and that's exactly why your parents signed you up.

Sometimes it's really good for us to get away from all our things and just live in a simpler and more different way than we are used to- so that we can appreciate everything that we do have.

So...homesickness is our body's natural reaction to missing the comforts that we are used to having in our life. This is called our COMFORT ZONE- the area where we live that is comfortable to us.

Homesickness feels uncomfortable because it can sometimes cause our bodies to feel achey and nauseous. It can make us tired and restless, because it's difficult to sleep when we are homesick. Also, we may have changes in our eating habits- we want to eat more or less than usual to try and comfort our bodies.

These are all temporary effects of homesickness and they can be easily treated. Usually, all these subside in a couple days with proper sleep and food. As soon as we learn to adapt to our new surroundings, we feel more comfortable with the people, places and situations that are new to us.

The physical effects of homesickness; like achiness in our body and being uncomfortable, are relatively easy to deal with- it's the emotional symptoms that are a little trickier.

Some of us feel these emotional symptoms of homesickness too. These can be feelings of LOSS, ANXIETY and LONELINESS.

Loss? Of what?
Well...loss of all the most important people and comforts in our life. It feels weird to think that the people in our life are living without us. It's hard for us not to feel bad for our family and friends who miss us... because if we are missing them, then they MUST be missing us too- that's sad isn't it? Yes...and no. It's really good for people who see each other all the time to spend a little time apart every once in a while...it gives us a chance to miss them and to appreciate how much we enjoy having them in our life. We can still have them with us even if they're not right beside us- a picture or a special object that reminds us of the special people and animals in our life helps miss them less.

Anxiety sounds like such a strange word, but it really just means when we STRESS and WORRY due to fear.

Stress is tension that our BODY feels when we are scared. Worry is a thought that we have in our MIND when we are scared.

Why STRESS when we are away from our comfort zone?

Well, it's a natural reaction for our body to feel stressed and a little afraid when we are placed in new situations. Its kind of scary to live somewhere new, around new people and things. What makes it scary is that we are not sure if we are safe or secure in these new places, because we've never been to them before. It's totally normal to have fear of the unknown... but don't worry- our body is prepared to deal with fear!

The body's reaction to fear is called the "FIGHT or FLIGHT" Response. Check out how it works on the next page...

The FIGHT Or FLIGHT Response?

Imagine you're a caveman or cavewoman living 100,000 years ago - and you come face to face with a hungry saber-toothed tiger. You have two choices: 1) Run for it (that's flight), or 2) pick up your club and battle the tiger (that's fight). A final choice (be eaten) doesn't seem like such a good one!

To prepare for fight or flight, your body does a number of things automatically so it's ready for quick action or a quick escape. Your heart rate increases to pump more blood to your muscles and brain. Your lungs take in air faster to supply your body with oxygen. The pupils in your eyes get larger to see better. And your digestive and urinary systems slow down for the moment so you can concentrate on more important things.

When we realize that our body doesn't need to face danger in these new situations, it's a lot easier to stay calm and ready to face new experiences and places- we don't have to be afraid!

So, even though our body instinctively prepares for danger, we can still calm down by breathing through each new situation. Try this the next time you feel stressed or a little anxious-

CLEAR YOUR MIND of all thoughts and try not to think of anything. Its difficult, so close your eyes if you like.
BREATHE in and out deeply and slowly to calm your body. Do this for a few minutes until you feel relaxed.
Now, open your eyes and NOTICE HOW YOU FEEL. Continue to clear your mind of all thoughts, but use your senses to discover how you feel. (Smell, touch, taste, hearing) What do you smell? Are you hungry or thirsty? Can you taste anything in your mouth? How does that taste make your body feel? Satisfied or more hungry? And so on...

Doing this quiets our mind so we can listen to our body, it helps us to understand how we feel. After having a few minutes to calm our body and mind, then we can RESPOND better to our stress instead of just reacting to our fear.

When you have to face being away from your comfort zone, like at a sleepover or even camp, there are ways to prepare your body for this ahead of time. When you prepare yourself, you can deal with the fear as slowly as you need to, instead of being forced to face it the moment it happens.

3Before you have to go away, wherever it is, here are some tips to help you prepare:
-If possible, visit the place ahead of time so that you will be familiar with it's surroundings
-Talk with family members about the upcoming separation
-Remember that it's normal to feel homesick
-Try a "practice" trip; a few days at a friend's or relative's house
-Write letters to yourself and ask your family to do this too before leaving- you will get them on your arrival to the place your going
-Encourage yourself to make friends and seek support from trusted adults when you get there
-Be enthusiastic and optimistic about your upcoming time away-from-home experience.
-Get prestamped, preaddressed envelopes and notebook paper from family members to write to them while you're away.

So, we know about stress...but, why WORRY when we are away from our comfort zone? If worry is just thoughts we have when we are scared of something, then these can be easily changed. All thoughts and feelings we have are so important, but we can change them at any time to make ourselves feel better!

When going away, fear is really common-what all humans are basically afraid of is being alone. When we leave our comfort zone, we are out there living in the unknown and it can feel like we are alone.

BUT WE'RE NOT...no matter where we go- there will be someone else there, someone else who can listen to our fears and someone else who may even be feeling the same way. A big part of feeling safe and comfortable is being around other people- people who remind us that we are loved; like family and friends.

Sometimes, we have to make OTHER families wherever we go, if we cant be around the one that we have at home. We can have so many families- at home, at school, on sports teams and in our activity clubs. All these other families make our experiences outside our home just as comfortable. So, no worries-YOUR NOT ALONE...and if your going away...

...try to go BEYOND YOUR COMFORT ZONE!

Cures for Homesickness

Bring a little bit of home with you.
If you're going away from home, bring your pillow or your favorite pajamas. You also can bring pictures of the people you'll be apart from and look at them any time you want.

Keep busy.
The more fun stuff you do, the less time you'll have to feel homesick. Try to join in activities wherever you are. If you're at camp, sign up for that kayak race and be sure to go to the Friday night dance. At a sleepover, play the games and do all the crazy dances! Even if you're not completely into it at first, you might soon start to have a good time.

Talk to someone where you are.
Sometimes, just telling someone that you're feeling a little homesick will help you feel better. If you're at camp, a camp counselor would be a good person to talk with. He or she might have some ideas to help you feel better.

Adapted from kidshealth.org (for more cures visit this site)

Essential Homesickness Sites

For Parents
acacamps.org
campparents.org
metroparent.com
pbs.org/parents

****FOR KIDS****
kidshealth.org
pbskids.org

****

Resources Used In This Book

1 Each year more than 11 million children and adults (staff members) attend camp in the U.S.-acacamps.org
2 Adapted From kidshealth.org
3 Adapted from webmd.com

*Special Thanks and Acknowledgements to the above websites. All of these offer helpful information, highly recommended!

A Message From The Author...

I have to admit that I have a little social anxiety- I love being out in public and seeing people...but the THOUGHT of going somewhere away from my home makes me feel a little nervous and uneasy. I'm not shy, I can walk into any room full of people and talk to someone with no problem-I just have difficulty when I think about it- the thought makes me afraid. So.....I try to just get out there WITHOUT playing out the "mind chatter" in my head or worrying about how it's going to go, before I do it! If I didn't just do it, then I would never get out of my comfort zone and I'de never have the chance to meet great people and experience new things! To me, being a little uncomfortable is worth not missing out on these wonderful things about life! Good Luck!
Tracy

A Special Dedication To...All My Camp Counselors!

Camp was some of the best summers of my life- I got to be a camper and a counselor at several different camps. My first summer was scary(or so I thought it would be before I went) This fear left me probably after the second smore that I popped into my mouth! Actually, I had a fantastic couselor my first year who made me feel so comfortable about our cabin (the place where her and I would be sleeping and relaxing in, along with the other girls in my group that she was in charge of). She told me to think of the cabin kind of as our house. All of us were a little family that watched out for each other. No one was left alone, so we could feel safe and when we were all comfortable with each other, we could talk and share our feelings, just like a real family. I thought this was great and I saw her more as the really cool babysitter that got to stay over at my house for longer than one night! Thank you to my first counselor and all of them that I was lucky to have- in some of the best summers of my life!

46172804R00024